The BIG Aqua Book of Beginner Books

The BIG Aqua Book of

Beginner Books

By Dr. Seuss, Robert Lopshire,
and Al Perkins

Illustrated by Dr. Seuss, Art Cummings,
Robert Lopshire, and Eric Gurney

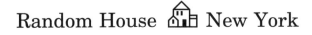

Random House 🏠 New York

Dr. Seuss's real name was Theodor Geisel. On books he wrote to be illustrated by others, he often used the name Theo. LeSieg, which is Geisel spelled backward.

Contents

The BIG Aqua Book of Beginner Books

There's a WOCKET in my POCKET !

By Dr. Seuss

Did you
ever have the feeling
there's a
WASKET
in your
BASKET?

. . . Or a NUREAU
in your BUREAU?

. . . Or a WOSET in your CLOSET?

Sometimes
I feel quite CERTAIN
   there's a JERTAIN
      in the CURTAIN.

Sometimes
I have the feeling
there's a ZLOCK
behind the CLOCK.

And that ZELF
up on that SHELF!

I have
talked to him
myself.

That's the
kind of house
I live in.

There's a NINK
in the SINK.

And a
ZAMP
in the
LAMP.

And they're
rather nice
. . . I think.

Some of them
are very friendly.

Like the
YOT
in the
POT.

But
that
YOTTLE
in
the
BOTTLE!

Some are friendly.
Some are NOT.

I like the
ZABLE
on the
TABLE.

And the
GHAIR under the CHAIR.

But that BOFA
   on the SOFA . . .

Well,
I wish
he wasn't there.

All those NUPBOARDS
in the CUPBOARDS.

They're good fun
to have about.

But that
NOOTH GRUSH
on my
TOOTH BRUSH . . .

Him
I could
do without!

The only one
I'm really scared of
is   that   VUG
under the RUG.

And that QUIMNEY
up the CHIMNEY . . .

I don't like him.
Not at all.

And it makes me sort of nervous
when the ZALL scoots down the HALL.

But the YEPS
on the STEPS—

They're great fun
to have around.

And so are
many, many
other friends
that I have found. . . .

31

. . . Like the TELLAR
and the NELLAR
and the GELLAR
and the DELLAR
and the BELLAR
and the WELLAR
and the ZELLAR
in the CELLAR.

. . . And the GEELING
on the CEILING . . .

. . . and
the
ZOWER
in
my
SHOWER . . .

. . . and the ZILLOW
  on my PILLOW.

     I don't care
     if you believe it.
     That's the kind of house
     I live in.
     And I hope
     we never leave it.

HAND, HAND, FINGERS, THUMB

BY AL PERKINS

ILLUSTRATED BY ERIC GURNEY

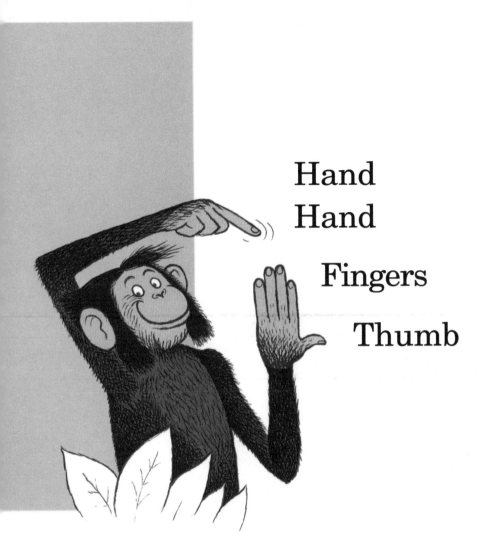

Hand
Hand

Fingers

Thumb

One thumb
One thumb
Drumming on a drum.

One hand
Two hands
Drumming on a drum.

Dum ditty
Dum ditty
Dum dum dum.

Rings on fingers.

Rings on thumb.

Drum drum
Drum drum
Drum drum drum.

Monkeys drum . . .

. . . and monkeys hum.

Hum drum
Hum drum
Hum drum hum.

Hand picks an apple.

Hand picks a plum.

Dum ditty
Dum ditty
Dum dum dum.

Monkeys come
And monkeys go.

Hands with handkerchiefs.
Blow! Blow! Blow!

"Hello Jack."

"Hello Jake."

Shake hands
Shake hands
Shake! Shake! Shake!

"Bye-bye Jake."

"Bye-bye Jack."

Dum ditty
Dum ditty

Whack! Whack! Whack!

Hands play banjos
Strum strum strum.

Hands play fiddles
Zum zum zum.

Dum ditty
Dum ditty
Dum dum dum,

Hand in hand
More monkeys come.

Many more fingers.
Many more thumbs.
Many more monkeys.
Many more drums.

63

Millions of fingers!
Millions of thumbs!
Millions of monkeys
Drumming on drums!

Dum
ditty
Dum
ditty
Dum
dum
dum.

The CAT in the HAT COMES BACK!

By Dr. Seuss

This was no time for play.

This was no time for fun.

This was no time for games.

There was work to be done.

All that deep,

Deep, deep snow,

All that snow had to go.

When our mother went
Down to the town for the day,
She said, "Somebody has to
Clean all this away.
Somebody, SOMEBODY
Has to, you see."
Then she picked out two Somebodies.
Sally and me.

Well . . .
There we were.
We were working like that
And then who should come up
But the CAT IN THE HAT!

"Oh-oh!" Sally said.

"Don't you talk to that cat.

That cat is a bad one,

That Cat in the Hat.

He plays lots of bad tricks.

Don't you let him come near.

You know what he did

The last time he was here."

"Play tricks?" laughed the cat.

"Oh, my my! No, no, no!

I just want to go in

To get out of the snow.

Keep your mind on your work.

You just stay there, you two.

I will go in the house

And find something to do."

Then that cat went right in!

He was up to no good!

So I ran in after

As fast as I could!

Do you know where I found him?

You know where he was?

He was eating a cake in the tub!

Yes he was!

The hot water was on

And the cold water, too.

And I said to the cat,

"What a bad thing to do!"

"But I like to eat cake

In a tub," laughed the cat.

"You should try it some time,"

Laughed the cat as he sat.

And then I got mad.
This was no time for fun.
I said, "Cat! You get out!
There is work to be done.
I have no time for tricks.
I must go back and dig.
I can't have you in here
Eating cake like a pig!
You get out of this house!
We don't want you about!"
Then I shut off the water
And let it run out.

The water ran out.

And then I SAW THE RING!

A ring in the tub!

And, oh boy! What a thing!

A big long pink cat ring!

It looked like pink ink!

And I said, "Will this ever

Come off? I don't think!"

"Have no fear of that ring,"
Laughed the Cat in the Hat.
"Why, I can take cat rings
Off tubs. Just like that!"

Do you know how he did it?
WITH MOTHER'S WHITE DRESS!
Now the tub was all clean,
But her dress was a mess!

Then Sally looked in.

Sally saw the dress, too!

And Sally and I

Did not know what to do.

We should work in the snow.

But that dress! What a spot!

"It may never come off!"

Sally said. "It may not!"

But the cat laughed, "Ho! Ho!
I can make the spot go.
The way I take spots off a dress
Is just so!"

"See here!" laughed the cat.

"It is not hard at all.

The thing that takes spots

Off a dress is a wall!"

Then we saw the cat wipe

The spot off the dress.

Now the dress was all clean.

But the wall! What a mess!

"Oh, wall spots!" he laughed.
"Let me tell you some news.
To take spots off a wall,
All I need is two shoes!"

Whose shoes did he use?
I looked and saw whose!
And I said to the cat,
"This is very bad news.
Now the spot is all over
DAD'S $10 SHOES!"

"But your dad will not
Know about that,"
Said the cat.
"He will never find out,"
Laughed the Cat in the Hat.
"His $10 shoes will have
No spots at all.
I will rub them right off
On this rug in the hall."

"But now we have rug spots!"
I yelled. "What a day!
Rug spots! What next?
Can you take THEM away?"

"Don't ask me," he laughed.

"Why, you know that I can!"

Then he picked up the rug

And away the cat ran.

"I can clean up these rug spots
Before you count three!
No spots are too hard
For a Hat Cat like me!"

He ran into Dad's bedroom
And then the cat said,
"It is good that your dad
Has the right kind of bed."

Then he shook the rug!

CRACK!

Now the bed had the spot!

And all I could say was,

"Now what, Cat?

NOW what?"

But the cat just stood still.

He just looked at the bed.

"This is NOT the right kind of a bed,"

The cat said.

"To take spots off THIS bed

Will be hard," said the cat.

"I can't do it alone,"

Said the Cat in the Hat.

"It is good I have some one
To help me," he said.
"Right here in my hat
On the top of my head!
It is good that I have him
Here with me today.
He helps me a lot.
This is Little Cat A."

And then Little Cat A

Took the hat off HIS head.

"It is good I have some one

To help ME," he said.

"This is Little Cat B.

And I keep him about,

And when I need help

Then I let him come out."

And then B said,

"I think we need Little Cat C.

That spot is too much

For the A cat and me.

But now, have no fear!

We will clean it away!

The three of us! Little Cats B, C and A!"

"Come on! Take it away!"
Yelled Little Cat A.

"I will hit that old spot
With this broom! Do you see?
It comes off the old bed!
It goes on the T.V."

And then Little Cat B
Cleaned up the T.V.

He cleaned it with milk,
Put the spot in a pan!
And then C blew it out
Of the house with a fan!

"But look where it went!"
I said. "Look where it blew!
You blew the mess
Out of the house. That is true.
But now you made Snow Spots!
You can't let THEM stay!"

"Let us think about that now,"
Said C, B and A.

"With some help, we can do it!"
Said Little Cat C.
Then POP! On his head
We saw Little Cat D!
Then, POP! POP! POP!
Little Cats E, F and G!

"We will clean up that snow
If it takes us all day!
If it takes us all night,
We will clean it away!"
Said Little Cats G, F, E, D, C, B, A.

They ran out of the house then
And we ran out, too.
And the Big Cat laughed,
"Now you will see something new!
My cats are all clever.
My cats are good shots.
My cats have good guns.
They will kill all those spots!"

But this did not look

Very clever to me.

Kill snow spots with pop guns?

That just could not be!

"All this does is make MORE spots!"

We yelled at the cat.

"Your cats are no good.

Put them back in your hat.

"Take your Little Cats G,
F, E, D, C, B, A.
Put them back in your hat
And you take them away!"

"Oh, no!" said the cat.
"All they need is more help.
Help is all that they need.
So keep still and don't yelp."

Then Little Cat G

Took the hat off his head.

"I have Little Cat H

Here to help us," he said.

"Little Cats H, I, J,

K, L and M.

But our work is so hard

We must have more than them.

We need Little Cat N.

We need O. We need P.

We need Little Cats Q, R, S, T,

U and V."

"Come on! Kill those spots!

Kill the mess!" yelled the cats.

And they jumped at the snow

With long rakes and red bats.

They put it in pails

And they made high pink hills!

Pink snow men! Pink snow balls!

And little pink pills!

Oh, the things that they did!

And they did them so hard,

It was all one big spot now

All over the yard!

But the Big Cat stood there

And he said, "This is good.

This is what they should do

And I knew that they would.

"With a little more help,
All the work will be done.
They need one more cat.
And I know just the one."

"Look close! In my hand
I have Little Cat V.
On his head are Cats W,
X, Y and Z."

"Z is too small to see.

So don't try. You can not.

But Z is the cat

Who will clean up that spot!"

"Now here is the Z
You can't see," said the Cat.
"And I bet you can't guess
What he has in HIS hat!

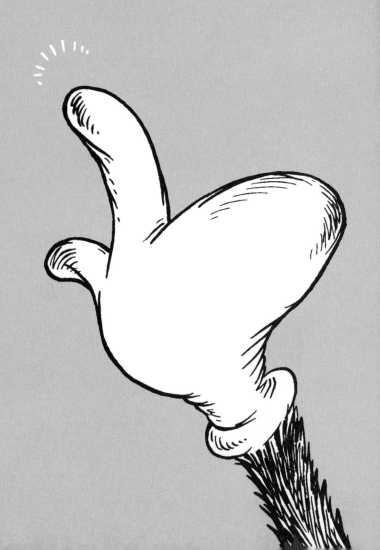

124

"He has something called VOOM.

Voom is so hard to get,

You never saw anything

Like it, I bet.

Why, Voom cleans up anything

Clean as can be!"

Then he yelled,

"Take your hat off now,

Little Cat Z!

Take the Voom off your head!

Make it clean up the snow!

Hurry! You Little Cat!

One! Two! Three! GO!"

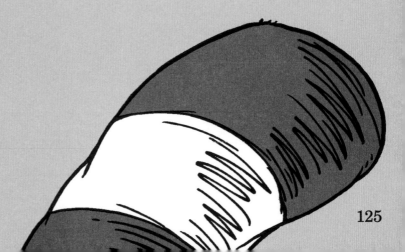

126

Then the Voom . . .

It went VOOM!

And, oh boy! What a VOOM!

Now, don't ask me what Voom is.

I never will know.

But, boy! Let me tell you

It DOES clean up snow!

"So you see!" laughed the Cat,

"Now your snow is all white!

Now your work is all done!

Now your house is all right!

And you know where my little cats are?"

Said the cat.

"That Voom blew my little cats

Back in my hat.

And so, if you ever

Have spots, now and then,

I will be very happy

To come here again . . .

"... with Little Cats A, B, C, D ...

E, F, G ...

H, I, J, K ...

L, M, N ...

and O, P ...

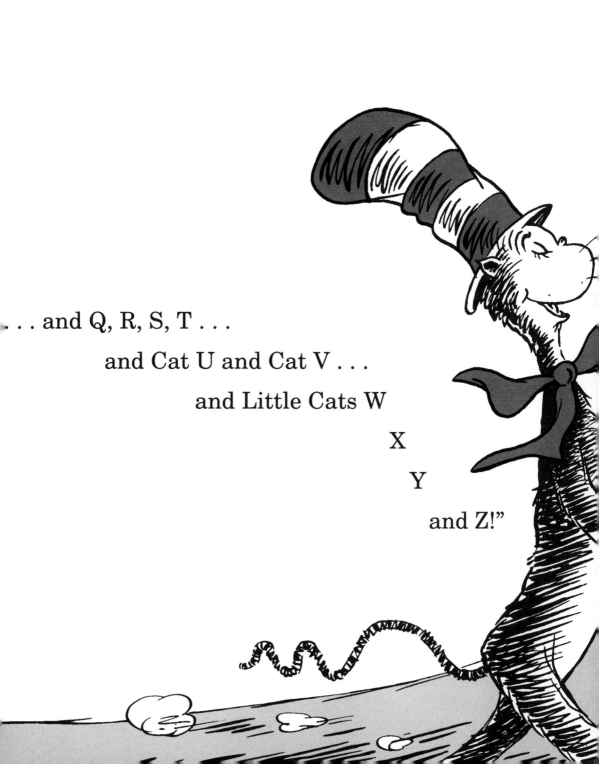

. . . and Q, R, S, T . . .

and Cat U and Cat V . . .

and Little Cats W

X

Y

and Z!"

New Tricks I Can Do!

Robert Lopshire

Hello there, Spot.

How do you do?

You don't look good . . .

What's wrong with you?

The circus said
that I must go.
They say most folks
have seen my show.

137

Folks saw my spots
up in the air.
Folks saw my spots
most everywhere.
The circus says
that's all I do.
The circus wants
somebody new.
But I have more
that I can do . . .
all kinds of tricks—
and all brand-new!

What are these tricks
you say are new?

Please show us some.

Oh yes, please do!

I'll show you both
a trick or two.
Like this one here
where I turn blue.
The circus folks
will say, Please stay,
when they see me
turn blue this way.

Or I can be
all red, you see.

Or I can be . . .

. . . a yellow me!

They'll like these tricks
that I can do.
And I have more
to show to you!

I can be green,

like this, you know . . .

. . . or violet
from head to toe.

These things are new
as new can be!
Can you do more?
If so, let's see!

152

I can make
each spot be square,
in any color
that I care. . . .
Those circus folks
will want me back,
when they see me
in squares of black.

I know that these
would please them too.
And so would . . .

Stripes!

In pink and blue!

And I have more
that I can do,
so watch me,
watch me now, you two . . .

As I do this—
and this is new—
I make myself
red, white, and blue!

And there is more,
much more I do,
so watch me now.
Watch, watch, you two!

159

Like this one here,
you'll like, I know . . .
when I do this
from top to toe!

161

Those circus folks
will like this one.
This kind of trick
is never done!

They'd take me back
if they just knew
all of the tricks
that I can do!

They'd take me back,
they'd be so glad,
if they saw me,
like this, in plaid.
The circus says
that I am through,
but I have more
that I can do!

165

166

Like this trick here
I've done for you.
It's just one more
that I can do.
Tell me, tell me
now, you two.
How do you like
the tricks I do?

With all the tricks
you've seen today,
will the circus ask
for me to stay?

GOLDSMITH
The
JUGGLER

DINGLE BROTHERS
CIRCUS
BRINGS YOU

SPOT
And His Spots!

We like these tricks
that you can do,
but the circus is
all wrong for you!
With tricks this good,
you need to be
where folks can see you . . .

. . . on TV!

Said a book-reading parrot named Hooey,

"The words in this book are all phooey.

When you say them, your lips

will make slips and back flips

and your tongue may end up in Saint Looey!"

Do you like fresh fish?
It's just fine at Finney's Diner.
Finney also has some fresher fish
that's fresher and much finer.
But his best fish is his freshest fish
and Finney says with pride,
"The finest fish at Finney's
is my freshest fish, French-fried!"

SO . . .
don't order the fresh
or the fresher fish.
At Finney's, if you're wise,
you'll say,
"Fetch me the finest
French-fried freshest
fish that Finney fries!"

Dinn's Shin

We have a dinosaur named Dinn.

Dinn's thin. Dinn doesn't have much skin.

And the bones fall out

of his left front shin.

Then we have to call in Pinner Blinn,
who comes with his handy shin-pin bin
and with a thin Blinn shinbone pin,
Blinn pins Dinn's shinbones right back in.

Bed Spreaders spread spreads on beds.

Bread Spreaders spread butters on breads.

And that Bed Spreader better

watch out how he's spreading . . .

or that Bread Spreader's
sure going to butter his bedding.

Ape Cakes
Grape Cakes

As he gobbled the cakes on his plate,
the greedy ape said as he ate,
"The greener green grapes are,
the keener keen apes are
to gobble green grape cakes.
They're GREAT!"

Are you having trouble
in saying this stuff?
It's really quite easy for me.
I just look in my mirror
and see what I say,
and then I just say what I see.

Now let's talk about MONEY!

You should leave your Grox home
when you travel by air.
If you take him along,
they charge double the fare.
And your Grox must be packed
and locked up in a Grox Box,
which costs much, much more
than a little old fox box.
So it's heaps a lot cheaper
to fly with your foxes
than waste all that money
on boxes for Groxes.

And, what do you think costs more? . . .

A Simple Thimble

or

a Single Shingle?

A simple thimble <u>could</u> cost less
than a single shingle would, I guess.
So I think that the single shingle <u>should</u>
cost more than the simple thimble would.

If you like to eat potato chips

and chew pork chops on clipper ships,

I suggest that you chew

a few chips and a chop

at Skipper Zipp's Clipper Ship Chip Chop Shop.

And if your tongue
is getting queasy,
don't give up.
The next one's EASY!

There are so many things
that you really should know.
And that's why I'm bothering
telling you so.
You should know the first names
of the Fuddnuddler Brothers
who like to pile each on the heads of the others.
If you start at the top,
there are Bipper and Bud
and Skipper and Jipper
and Jeffrey and Jud,
Horatio, Horace and Hendrix and Hud,
and then come Dinwoodie and Dinty and Dud,
also Fitzsimmon and Frederick and Fud,
and Slinkey and Stinkey and Stuart and Stud.
And, down at the bottom
is poor little Lud.
But if Lud ever sneezes,
his name will be MUD.

We have two ducks. One blue. One black.
And when our blue duck goes "Quack-quack"
our black duck quickly quack-quacks back.
The quacks Blue quacks make her quite a quacker
but Black is a quicker quacker-backer.

AND . . . speaking of quacks
reminds me of cracks
and stacks and sacks
and shacks and Schnacks.
SO . . . oh say can you say,
"I have cracks in my shack,
I have smoke in my stack,
and I think there's a Schnack
in the sack on my back!"

Upon an island hard to reach,

the East Beast sits upon his beach.

Upon the west beach sits the West Beast.

Each beach beast thinks he's the best beast.

EAST BEAST

Which beast is best? . . . Well, I thought at first
that the East was best and the West was worst.
Then I looked again from the west to the east
and I liked the beast on the east beach least.

195

Pete Pats Pigs

Pete Briggs pats pigs.

Briggs pats pink pigs.

Briggs pats big pigs.

(Don't ask me why. It doesn't matter.)

Pete Briggs is a pink pig, big pig patter.

Pete Briggs pats his big pink pigs all day.

(Don't ask me why. I cannot say.)

Then Pete puts his patted pigs away

in his Pete Briggs' Pink Pigs Big Pigs Pigpen.

Fritz needs Fred and Fred needs Fritz.

Fritz feeds Fred and Fred feeds Fritz.

Fred feeds Fritz with ritzy Fred food.

Fritz feeds Fred with ritzy Fritz food.

And Fritz, when fed, has often said,

"I'm a Fred-fed Fritz.

Fred's a Fritz-fed Fred."

How to tell a Klotz from a Glotz

Well, the Glotz, you will notice,
has lots of black spots.
The Klotz is quite different
with lots of black dots.
But the big problem is
that the spots on a Glotz
are about the same size
as the dots on a Klotz.
So you first have to spot
who the one with the dots is.
Then it's easy to tell
who the Klotz or the Glotz is.

What would you rather be when you Grow Up?

A cop in a cop's cap?

Or a cupcake cook
in a cupcake cook's cap?

Or a fat flapjack flapper
in a flat flapped-jack cap?

OR . . .
if you think
you don't like cops' caps,
flapjack flappers'
or cupcake cooks' caps,
maybe you're one
of those choosy chaps
who likes kooky captains' caps
perhaps.

Well, when Blinn comes home tired
from his work pinning shins,
the happiest hour of old Blinn's day begins.
Mr. Blinn is the father of musical twins
who, tucking twin instruments under twin chins,
lull their daddy to sleep with twin Blinn violins.

204

AND . . . oh say can you say,
"Far away in Berlin
a musical urchin named Gretchen von Schwinn
has a blue-footed, true-footed,
trick-fingered, slick-fingered,
six-fingered, six-stringed tin Schwinn mandolin."

Rope Soap
Hoop Soap

If you hope

to wash soup off a rope,

simply scrub it with SKROPE!

Skrope is so strong that no rope is too long!

But if you should wish to wash
soup off a hoop, I suggest that it's best
to let your whole silly souped-up hoop soak
in Soapy Cooper's Super Soup-Off-Hoops Soak Suds.

One year we had a Christmas brunch
with Merry Christmas Mush to munch.
But I don't think you'd care for such.
We didn't like to munch mush much.

And, speaking of Christmas...

Here are
some Great Gifts
to give to your daddy!

If your daddy's name is Jim
and if Jim swims and if Jim's slim,
the perfect Christmas gift for him
is a set of Slim Jim Swim Fins.

But if your daddy's name is Dwight
and he likes to look at birds at night,
the gift for Dwight that might be right
is a Bright Dwight Bird-Flight
Night-Sight Light.

But Never Give Your Daddy a Walrus

A walrus with whiskers
is not a good pet.
And a walrus which whispers
is worse even yet.
When a walrus lisps whispers
through tough rough wet whiskers,
your poor daddy's ear
will get blispers and bliskers.

And that's almost enough
of such stuff for one day.
One more and you're finished.
Oh say can you say? . . .

"The storm starts
when the drops start dropping.
When the drops stop dropping
then the storm starts stopping."

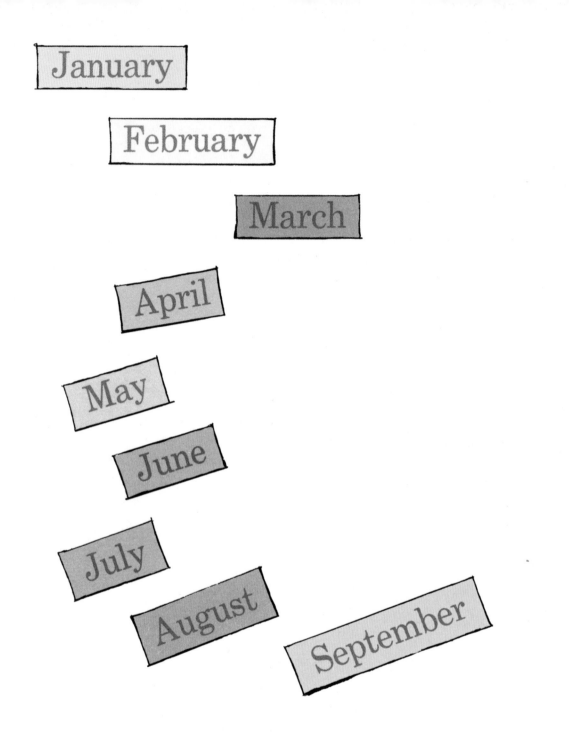

illustrated by Art Cumings

October

November

December

Please Try
to Remember
the **FIRST** of
OCTEMBER!

OCTEMBER

By **Dr. Seuss***

***writing as** Theo. LeSieg

Everyone wants

a big green kangaroo.

Maybe, perhaps,
you would like
to have TWO.

I want you to have them.
I'll buy them for you . . .

. . . if you'll wait

till the First of Octember.

Everyone wants
a new skateboard TV.
Some people want two.
And some people want three.

Perhaps you want four?

Well, that's OK with me . . .

. . . if you'll wait

till the First of Octember.

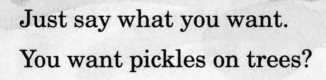

Just say what you want.
You want pickles on trees?

Want to swing
through the air
on a flying trapeze?

Just say what you want,
and whatever you say,
you'll get
on October the First.

WHAT A DAY!

When October comes round,
you can play a hot tune
on your very expensive
new Jook-a-ma-Zoon!

I wish you could play it
in May or in June.

But May is too early.
And June is too soon.

When October gets here,
no work! And no school!

We'll build you a playhouse!
We'll build you a pool!
We would build t[...]
right now,
but right now
is too cool.

d we'll buy you

vonderful

ep-a-Fly kite!

hem

We will!

If you'll wait

till the month is just right.

Octember's the best
because March is too dusty.
And April won't do
because April's too gusty.

What <u>more</u> do you want?

Do you and your dog
want more time to relax? . . .
Less time on your feet
and more time on your backs? . . .
More time in the air
and less time on the ground? . . .

You'll get it
as soon as
Octember comes round.

Want to take a great trip?
Well, I know a great ship!

It sails
to Alaska,
Nebraska and Sweden,
making stops
in Ga-Dopps
and the Garden of Eden.

And it sails on the First of Octember!

What <u>else</u> do you want?

Want to play a new sport?

In October
we'll build you
a Hock-Zocker court!

239

You'll get all that you want.
You just write out your list.
<u>Everyone</u> has an October First list.

Write slowly now!
Don't break your wrist.

Then one of these days
the October First van
will drive up to your house
just as fast as it can.

Whatever you want,
you will get in big bags,
and boxes and crates
with your name on the tags.

You'll have
rockets to shoot.

You'll have
bombs you can burst . . .

244

. . . on the wonderful
night of

**OCTEMBER
THE
FIRST!**

246

On the First of Octember
you'll stay up all night,
drinking 66 six-packs
of Doodle Delight.

Whatever
you ask for,
I want
you to get.

But October—

I'm sorry—

just isn't <u>here</u> yet.

SO . . .
Be sure
to be here.
Be sure you're in town
on Octember the First . . .

. . . when
the
money
comes
down!

It doesn't
come down much
in March
or November—
or even September . . .

. . . or in August,
October,
July
or December.

But
EVERYTHING'S
YOURS . . .

. . . on the First
of Octember!

On the First
of Octember?

Thank <u>you</u>!
I'll remember.